Euclid Bunny
Delivers the Mail

BRUCE KOSCIELNIAK

ALFRED A. KNOPF : NEW YORK

For Betty Lou Zajac

Day was breaking on the Barnyard post office.

All the chickens who deliver the Barnyard mail were down with the flu. And the post office was filled to the rafters with letters and packages waiting to be delivered.

"Whatever will we do?" groaned postmaster Bernie Bear.
"Pretend there's no mail?" sighed Fluffy Fowl.
"Let's call Euclid Bunny Speedy Delivery Service!" clucked Muffy Hen.
"Dial the number," said Bernie.

"Hello? Euclid Bunny? Bernie Bear here. We've got a little problem at the post office this morning. Can you help us?"

Quick as a bunny, Euclid was there.

"Here's the delivery route. Take this map. You should be back in three or four hours," said Bernie. "And make sure you get the out-of-town mail to the station for the three o'clock train. Got it?"

"I'm out of here," chimed the speedy bunny.

BARNYAR

BARNYARD POST OFFICE

MOUSE FIELD

BARNYARD RAILWAY STATION
3 P.M. TRAIN

Bunny quick, Euclid loaded all the mail into his truck,
and off he went. First he stopped at the mouse field.

Then he sped through the cow pasture.

He breezed by the duck pond.

And skipped past the pig farm.
"What was that?" asked Penny Pig.

Then Euclid delivered all the mail for the
deer and the moose.

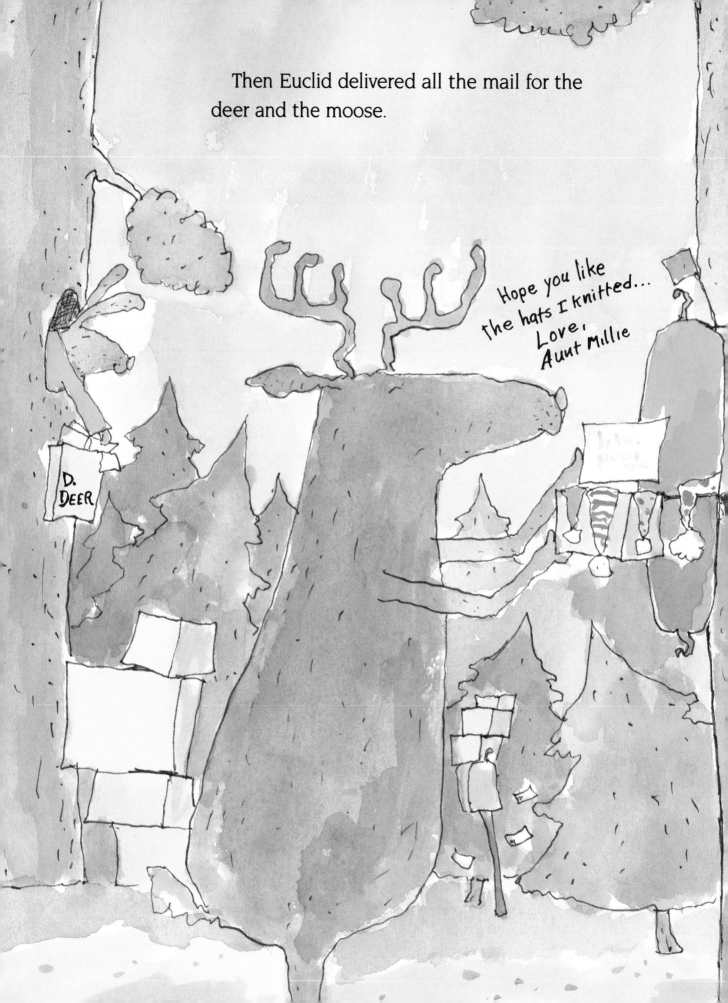

This is too easy, he thought as he hopped about his business.

In a twitch he was scooting up to the squirrels' nest.

And down to the owls'.

"Yikes!" muttered Euclid, "there's the train for the out-of-town mail. I'd better step on it."

And with the mail safely on the train, Euclid raced back to the Barnyard post office.

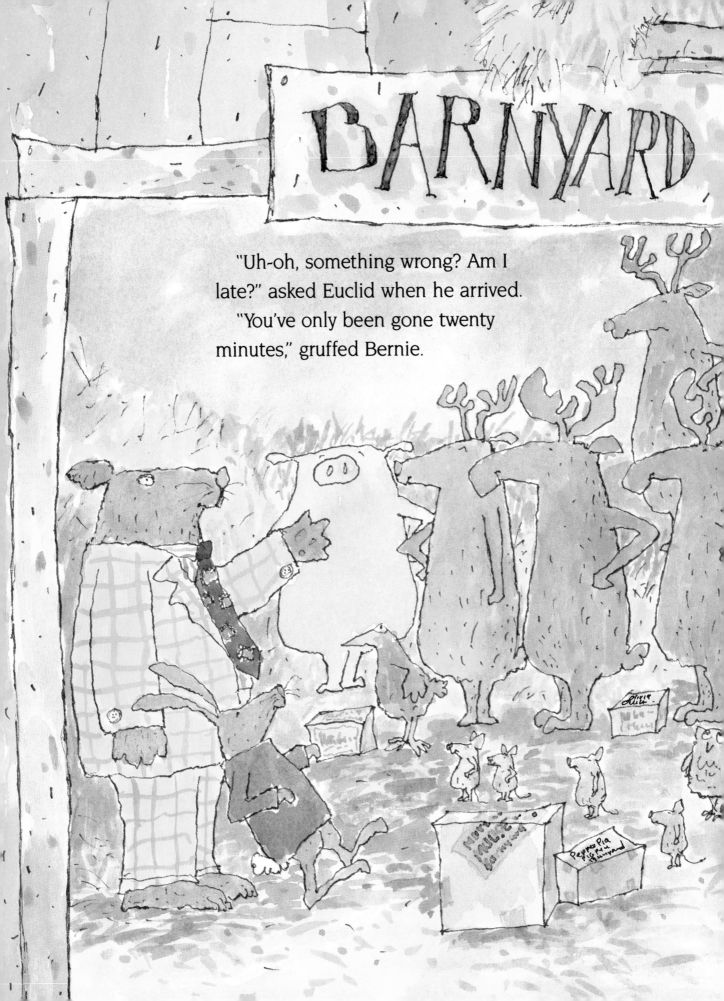

"Uh-oh, something wrong? Am I late?" asked Euclid when he arrived. "You've only been gone twenty minutes," gruffed Bernie.

But something *was* wrong. Mortimer Moose had gotten a TV that should have gone to Murray Mouse. Donny and Dotty Mouse had gotten a refrigerator meant for Danny and Dorry Deer.

Scotty Squirrel had gotten Pomeroy Pig's golf clubs. Roland Reindeer had gotten six hats addressed to Dubber and Dilly Duck's ducklings.

Percy Pig got Monty Moose's bath soap. And Durwin
Duck got a postcard from "Mom and Dad"—Betty and Bruno Bear.

Chloe Cow got someone's tiny tea service. And Olivia Owl
got Penny Pig's umbrella stand.

"Seems like you were a bit too hasty," growled
Bernie Bear. "Now what are we going to do?"
"Oooh, don't worry. I'll take care of it," said Euclid.

Bunny quick, he hopped around the Barnyard post
office sorting the mail.

And when everything landed,

everyone had the right things.

"Call me if you ever need help again," said Euclid.
"Maybe," said Bernie. "Hey, wait a minute. There's a
letter here addressed to Euclid Bunny."

Dear Euclid,

We just got a call from Benny, the Barnyard Easter Bunny, who's down with the flu. Looks like you'll have to deliver the Barnyard Easter eggs this year, Sonny. So hotfoot it home and bring lots of eggs!

Love,
Granny Bunny

Quick as a bunny, Euclid was gone.

THIS IS A BORZOI BOOK PUBLISHED BY ALFRED A. KNOPF, INC.

Book design by Mina Greenstein

Manufactured in the United States of America

2   4   6   8   10   9   7   5   3   1

Library of Congress Cataloging-in-Publication Data

Koscielniak, Bruce.

Euclid Bunny delivers the mail / by Bruce Koscielniak.

p.   cm. Summary: When the chickens who deliver the Barnyard mail come down with the flu,
postmaster Bernie Bear hires a speedy bunny to do the job, with humorous results.

ISBN 0-679-81069-2 (trade)   ISBN 0-679-91069-7 (lib. bdg.)

[1. Postal service—Letter carriers—Fiction. 2. Animals—Fiction.]   I. Title.   PZ7.K8523Eu   1991

[E]—dc20   90-4696   CIP   AC